LIGHT-FINGERED
LARRY

Jan Fearnley

EGMONT

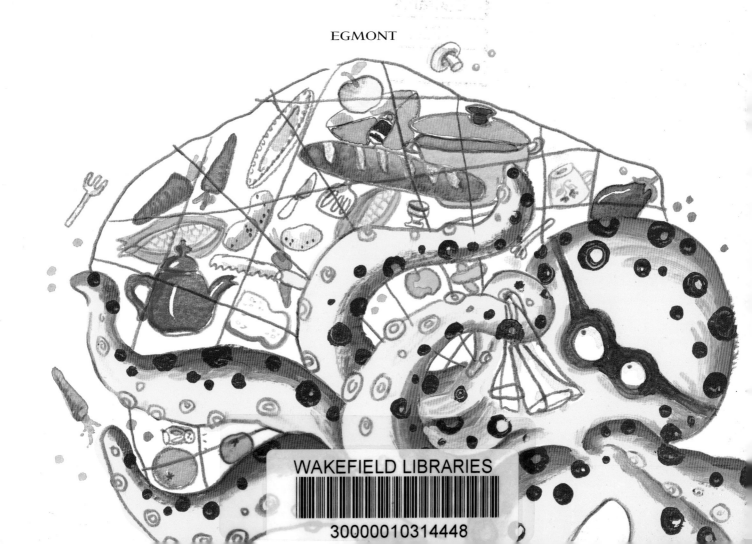

WANTED!

HAVE YOU SEEN THIS NAUGHTY OCTOPUS?

Look under here!

EGMONT
We bring stories to life

First published in Great Britain 2014
by Egmont UK Limited
The Yellow Building, 1 Nicholas Road, London W11 4AN
www.egmont.co.uk

Text and illustrations copyright © Jan Fearnley 2014

Jan Fearnley has asserted her moral rights.

ISBN 978 1 4052 6538 6 (Paperback)

A CIP catalogue record for this book is available from the British Library.

For Ella, with love.

And in loving memory of
Kira
aka Kira Bagheera, Kira Steiff,
Kira Royale, Busty Chuckles, and
The Hooked Claw. Miss you so much,
my dearest friend. My drawing table is
not the same without you. xxx

Light-Fingered Larry was an octopus. He lived in the sea and he liked collecting things. Other people's things. He was a robber!

Every night, he slept on a bed of seaweed in his underwater den, surrounded by stolen treasure.

Every day, he went out, sneaking about,
taking things that weren't his and
putting them in his net of loot.

His eight arms were constantly
up to mischief.

If it wasn't tied down,
he'd **snatch** it!

If no one was looking, he'd **grab** it!

If it was there for the taking, he'd **nick** it!
Oh, he was a bad, bad octopus!

He stole Captain Rosie's washing off the line.

Nickity-nickity-nick-nick-GONE!

He pinched the Pond Children's jam tarts.

Nickity-nickity-nick-nick-GONE!

He snaffled
Boz the beaver's tools.

Nickity-nickity-nick-nick-GONE!

As slippery as you like, those sly tentacles
took things and stashed them away.

Now, Kiki Koala ran The Jolly Tugboat Inn.
Travellers came from far and wide to stay there,
and Kiki worked hard to make everybody happy.

One day, she was busy in the kitchen.

DING♪♪**-D⊙NG!**

went the bell at the desk, so Kiki went to answer it.

But somebody was watching . . .

As soon as Kiki was gone, up popped a sneaky tentacle
through the window, then another, then another . . .

Larry took the food, the pots,
the pans – the lot!

Nickity-nickity-nick-nick-
GONE! GONE! GONE!

But as he made off with her things,
Kiki came back.

"Stop! Thief!" she cried.

As fast as his tentacles could carry him,
Larry escaped with the loot.

"Somebody stop that octopus!"
squeaked Kiki.

Everybody came to help her.

Nickity-nickity-nick-nick–

GOTCHA!

Officer Pavani
locked Larry in jail.

"You'll stay here with me until you learn
not to be naughty," he said.

But Light-Fingered Larry had other ideas . . .

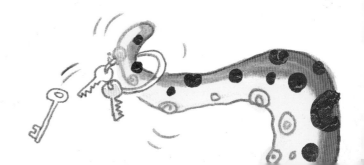

. . . with a slick sneaky move, he snatched the officer's keys,
let himself out and made his getaway!

STOP! cried Officer Pavani.

Larry grabbed the loot,
ran away and . . .

jumped into the sea.

Down and away he swam with his net of swag.
"Hee, hee," he chuckled. "They'll never catch me!"

Larry was feeling pretty clever.

Until . . .

. . . he got stuck!

Larry was snagged on the *Jaggedy Daggers!*

He was tangled there by his own bag of swag.

The animals held the end of the net
and pulled
and pulled
and

WHOOSH!

Up came the net, Larry and all the loot!

Larry was glad to be safe.
And he felt very sorry for what he'd done.

He gave back all of the things he'd taken.

And he did his best to make amends.

He noticed Kiki was very busy,
so he offered to help.

It turned out that Larry was
a natural in the kitchen!
Kiki was so impressed that
she gave him a job.

Larry didn't miss his robber's den. He had friends now, and to Larry friends were much more precious than any amount of stolen loot stashed at the bottom of the sea.

Larry gave everyone their things back.

Well, **nearly** everyone . . .

Officer Pavani never did find his missing keys,
because **somebody** was holding on to them,
just in case . . .